for
Jennifer
and
Michelle,
my inspirations

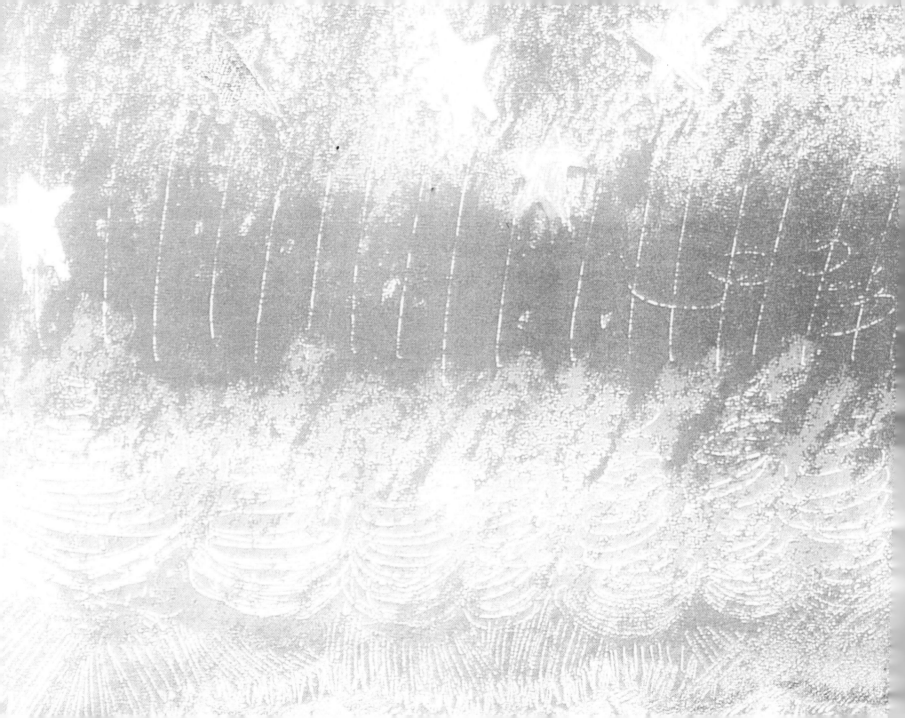

# ISTA CANTE

WRITTEN AND ILLUSTRATED BY
CAROLYN HAYES-KNOLL

Westview Publishing Co., Inc.
Nashville, Tennessee

The Eye of the Heart logo is a trademark of Carolyn Hayes-Knoll

First Edition November 2004

Printed in the United States

Layout and pre-press work by Westview Publishing Co., Inc.

™

Library of Congress Cataloging-in-Publication Data

Hayes-Knoll, Carolyn
  Ista Cante / written and illustrated by Carolyn Hayes-Knoll.-- 1st ed.
      p. cm.
  Summary: When a mother has a baby girl, she creates a special doll for her, made with the love and
fabric of many generations, who will love and encourage the daughter to grow to her full potential.
  ISBN 0-9755646-6-8 (alk. paper)
[1. Dolls--Fiction. 2. Mothers and daughters--Fiction.]  I. Title.
PZ7.H3148885Is 2004
[E]--dc22

                                      2004023542


               Published by Westview Publishing Co., Inc.
                    8120 Sawyer Brown Road, Suite 107
                         Nashville, TN  37221
                            (615) 646-8049
                      www.westviewpublishing.com

# I would like to acknowledge...

...my little mama, Margaret Stewart
for always believing in me.
Noa Ben-Amotz for her questioning
and guiding comments during the writing of this story.
June Zarwell, my mother, who never knew
her mother or her mother's mother,
and did not learn to know herself.

# ISTA CANTE

(ĭsh-tă chăn-tā)

eye of the heart

## INTUITION

ONCE THERE WAS AND
ONCE THERE WAS NOT....

ONCE THERE WAS AND ONCE THERE WAS NOT....

...a baby girl born to a mother who loved
her child as she loved the earth and sky,
as she loved the moon and stars,
as she loved herself.

The wise mother, knowing that she could
not always be with her child while she was
growing up, wanted to give her something
from within, something from her heart.

So the mother set to work,
sewing by hand, a doll;
a little life made from
scraps of material from
dresses her mother and
her mother's mother had made.

She had decided to name
the doll Ista Cante,
words meaning the
eye of the heart.
During quiet moments,
Ista Cante was created.
Each stitch became a prayer
for strength and love.

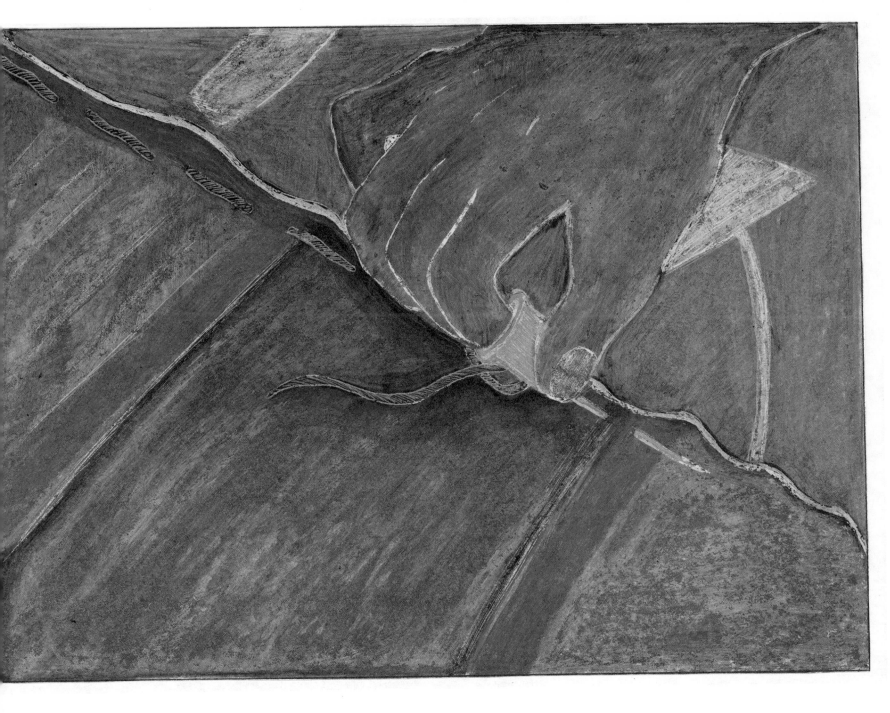

And within each piece of old material,
ancient memories and longings became
a part of each part of the doll.
As the last stitch was sewn
the mother knew that
a piece of her heart, her knowing,
some of who she was
breathed inside Ista Cante.

Holding the little doll close to her,
the contented mother walked over to
the cradle where her baby lay and
placed Ista Cante softly on her baby's
chest and spoke these words:

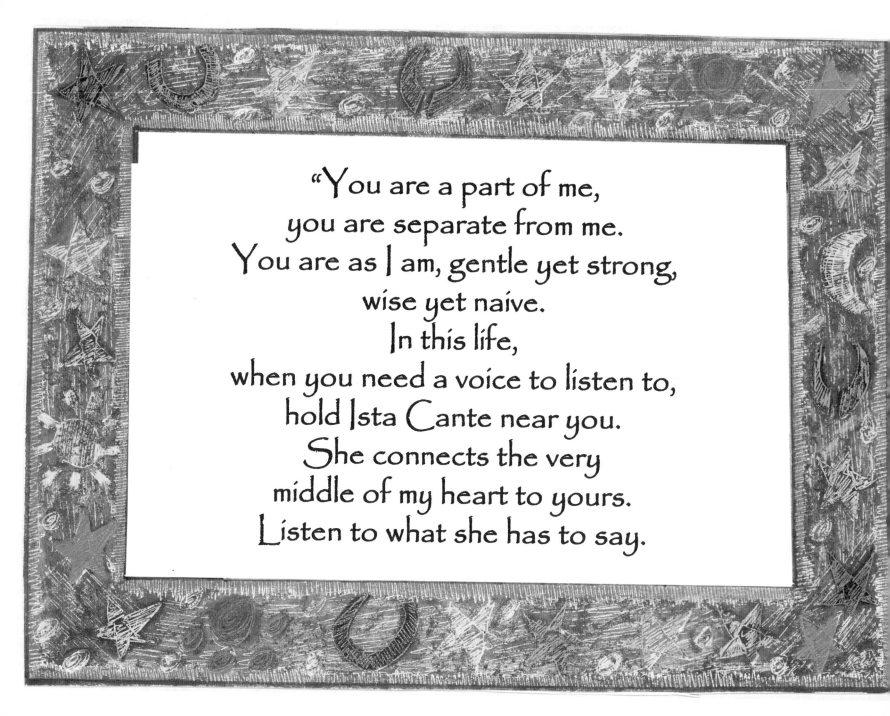

"You are a part of me,
you are separate from me.
You are as I am, gentle yet strong,
wise yet naïve.
In this life,
when you need a voice to listen to,
hold Ista Cante near you.
She connects the very
middle of my heart to yours.
Listen to what she has to say.

She will speak for me
when I am not able to
be with you.
And in time, you will find, my dear,
that your words and her thoughts
will become the same
and you will begin
to listen to your own
wise and intuitive thoughts."
And with that, she walked away.

As the child grew from a baby into a young girl, Ista Cante was her close companion. Sleeping and dreaming with her each night. Being lovingly carried each day. During play, the little girl pretended to feed Ista Cante. They would have imaginary conversations and, in turn, Ista Cante would feed the little girl's spirit.

In between running and resting,
tenderness, tears and time,
the child learned to
belong to herself always.

The mother began to see
in her daughter's eyes
a wise, wild and loving look
as if
she could see into and through life.

And while Ista Cante
became frayed and ragged,
the young girl became
strong and knowing.
The small life, the doll Ista Cante,
had accomplished her task.
The child grew into
a young woman who
listened to and trusted
her own inner voice.

And, in time, when
the child became a mother,
during quiet moments,
a small cloth doll
was stitched by hand,
for her baby,
from pieces of
her mother's and
her mother's mother's dresses.

Before my mother passed,
she said that, if it were possible, she would come back.
She hasn't come back in the way I had expected,
but within me and my daughters,
she is a part of me and of us.
She who created me is now within me.

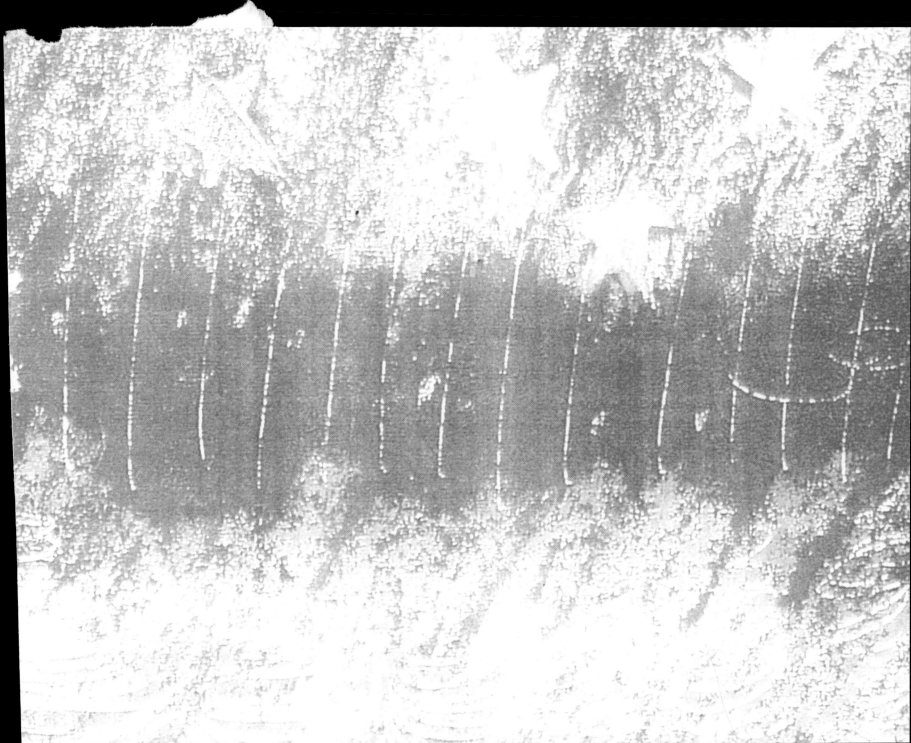

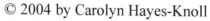